ON LINE

J
AMELIA
MOSS, MARISSA

AMELIA LENDS A HAND

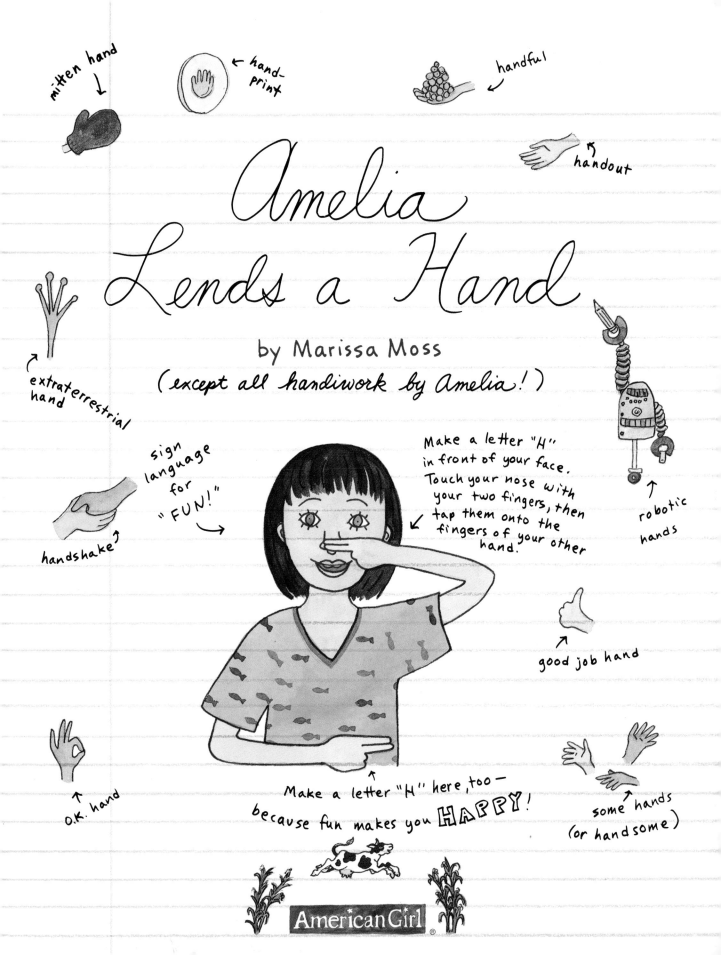

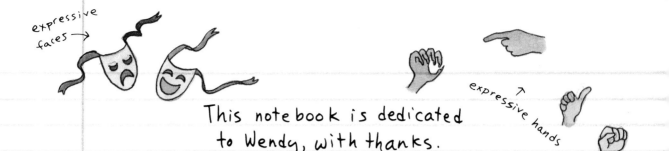

expressive faces →

expressive hands

This notebook is dedicated to Wendy, with thanks.

Pleasant Company Publications
8400 Fairway Place
Middleton, Wisconsin 53562

Book Design by Amelia
↰ de-sign or the sign?

← parachute guy

↑ parachute rocket

Library of Congress Cataloging-in-Publication Data
Moss, Marissa.
Amelia lends a hand / by Marissa Moss.
p. cm.
Summary: Amelia had expected to have a quiet summer, but instead she makes friends with a deaf boy who moves in next door, deals with her grouchy older sister, has an asthma attack, and goes to a family reunion. Features hand-printed text and drawings and thirty-two sign language flash cards.

ISBN 1-58485-508-8 (pbk.)   1-58485-539-8 (hc.)
[1. Deaf—Fiction. 2. Physically handicapped—Fiction.
3. Sign language—Fiction. 4. Sisters—Fiction.]
I. Title
PZ7.M8535 Ahk 2002
[Fic]—dc21   2001053405

pair o' shoes ↓

First Pleasant Company Publications printing, 2002
An Amelia® Book

American Girl® is a trademark of Pleasant Company.
Amelia® and the black-and-white notebook pattern are trademarks of Marissa Moss.
Manufactured in Singapore.

Cleo should take a DEEP breath and count backward before she BLOWS!

This is NOT the combination to my bike lock. →

02 03 04 05 06 07 08 TWP 10 9 8 7 6 5 4 3 2 1

0 1021 0154840 6

Summer is my favorite time of year, because it's so peaceful and quiet. Here's what you're supposed to hear:

ice cream truck music

buzzzzzzing bees

chirping birds

ice cracking in your glass of lemonade

Instead, all I hear this summer is Cleo fighting with Mom. Every little thing sets Cleo off — she's like a bomb, only there's no timer ticking off the seconds, so you never know when she'll blow. I try to stay out of it, but I can't help hearing them argue. I wish I could shut my ears!

Today started out pretty quiet, though. Cleo was at her best friend Gigi's house, and I was in the hammock watching the clouds and feeling the breeze tickle my toes, when I heard a

the Cleo explosive device

WHOOOOOSSH

and I saw a rocket — a little one, the kind I launched at Space Camp — soar way, way up.

It came from the backyard of our new neighbors. They moved in a couple of weeks ago, but I haven't met them yet. Mom took over some brownies as a "Welcome to our Neighborhood" kind of thing, but she hadn't said anything about them being rocket scientists.

When I looked in their yard, I saw a boy getting ready to launch another rocket.

He looked a little older than me, but not too much.

"Hey!" I yelled. "Hi, I'm Amelia, your neighbor. Can I set off a rocket? I know how — I've done it before."
The boy didn't answer me. He didn't even turn to look at me. I thought he was rude, or he hated girls, or he was a snob. He looked nice, but he wasn't.

Then another boy came out of the house — I figured he was Rocket Boy's little brother. The brother ran over to Rocket Boy, tugged on his sleeve, and moved his hands a lot, all without saying a word. That's when I got it — the boy with the rocket wasn't being rude — he was deaf. He couldn't hear me yelling at him.

The two of them went inside, and I spent the rest of the day thinking of how I could become friends with the deaf boy when I can't talk to him. Anyone who shoots off rockets is my kind of friend — I can't let his being deaf get in the way of being friends.

THWAAACK

SLAM!

The front door slammed. Cleo must be home — yep, I hear her snarling at Mom.

If I was deaf, I wouldn't hear Cleo being mad all the time. I wonder if deaf people feel lucky sometimes that they don't have to hear screaming.

Tonight at dinner I asked Mom what she knew about our neighbors.

The Rutellis? They're nice. They have three boys — one 15, one 11, and one 7. They go to your schools, except for the middle boy. He goes to a special school for deaf children.

Why do you care anyway, Amelia? Are you being nosy?

Just curious.

It was almost a normal, peaceful family meal.

No fights, just lots of loud chomping from Cleo.

In fact, it was such a normal dinner that Mom must have thought it was safe to make an announcement.

Guess what?

She didn't even wait for us to ask "what?"

I have some good news...

The way she said it, I had a feeling it was good for *her*, but not necessarily for us.

...something that will be a lot of fun...

Then she waited to see if Cleo and I were really listening. She knows our ears perk up when we hear "fun," but I could tell Cleo was suspicious of what Mom *meant* by fun.

I couldn't help remembering all the times Mom said something would be fun.

NEW KID NEW!

the first day in my new school

Putting my head underwater for the first time

being babysat by Mrs. Krapotnik

I could tell Cleo was thinking the same thing I was. Whenever a grown-up says something will be fun, BEWARE! But this time it didn't sound so bad. No dentist, no long hike, just a family reunion. Maybe not _fun_, but not torture, either. We're going to go to Uncle Leroy's farm next week to see all our aunts, uncles, and cousins.

Cleo, of course, hated the idea.

Mom tried to be nice, but she said no, only family was going this time, no friends. And the Cleo bomb went off.

So much for our normal dinner. I wrote to Nadia about it.
↓

Dear Nadia,
We're going to a family reunion
next week. Cleo hates the idea—
she exploded! But she's always
mad now anyway.
  The other news around here is our
new neighbor. He's just a little older
than me and shoots off rockets
in his backyard. I want to get
to know him. The problem is, he's
deaf, so I have to learn how to
talk to him first. Tomorrow I'm
going to the library, so I can try
to learn enough sign language
at least to say "Hi!"
       Yours till the ~~stop signs~~, Amelia

HAND SIGNALS
21¢

Nadia Kurz
61 South St.
Barton, CA
91010

↑
sign
of
finger-
pointing

I found a book on sign language, but it's a <u>lot</u>
more complicated than I thought. There are signs for
words and signs for the letters of the alphabet. I'm
starting with the ABC's — that's already plenty to
learn. If I get good at it, it will be like having a
secret code. Cleo will never be able to eavesdrop
on me and my new friend.

I'm drawing these with right hands because I'm right-handed, but
if you're left-handed, you'd use your left hand to sign.
↓

I'm trying
to learn
ASL or
American
Sign Language.
There are other
sign languages
(like signed
English),
but ASL
is the one
most deaf
people in
America use.

A   B   C   D   E   F   G

(Make a C
with your hand.)

(Curl your
fingers in.)

(Touch your
thumb to your
pointer finger.)

H   I   J   K   L   M   N

(Make an I,
then draw a hook
with it.)

(Put your
thumb
between the
two fingers.)

(Tuck your thumb
in so the tip sticks
out after the first
three fingers.)

(Here the
thumb tip
sticks out
after the
first two
fingers.)

O (Make an O with your hand.)

P (Like you're taking a pinch of something)

Q (Cross your fingers.)

R

S

T (Wiggle the T to say toilet.)

U

V (Like Little Bunny Foo Foo)

W

X

Y

Z (Draw a Z with your pointer finger.)

You ha<u>ve</u> to know the sign language alphabet so that when you don't know the sign for a word (or there isn't one — like for names), you can spell it out.

Today I got my chance to use sign language. I heard some noise from the Rutellis's yard, and, sure enough, the boy was there setting up his rockets. This time, I was prepared!

OPEN ME!

I threw a note folded into a paper airplane. It landed right at the boy's feet! He picked it up and read it, just like I'd hoped. Then he looked right at me— and smiled!

I knew he was nice!

He saluted me — that's how you say "Hi" in sign language. (I saw that in the book I checked out from the library.) I signed "Hi" back, but I didn't know what to sign after that.

The boy started signing words, but I couldn't understand ANYTHING! I shook my head, and he made a motion I <u>could</u> understand — he was telling me to come over, so I did.

First I got the rocket I brought home from Space Camp and then I climbed over the wall to show him. It would have taken me forever to spell out "launch the rocket," so I invented my own gestures to show what I meant.

Watch out! Thorny blackberries below!

And he understood! Between spelling things out and the gestures I made up, we could talk to each other—well, not really, but close enough.

Enzo, introducing himself to me — that's his name, Enzo Rutelli.

I've always thought hands are really expressive, with LOTS of personality. Enzo is proof of that. I love watching him sign because his whole body talks — not just his hands. I feel really clumsy next to him.

We launched rockets all afternoon. Sometimes it was hard because I could only say about 2% of what I meant. Lucky for me, Enzo's really patient when I'm slow at spelling things out. When it got <u>too</u> hard for me to understand, Enzo's little brother, Carlo, helped me out.

← I want to say something funny or smart, but I end up saying "I like rockets" over and over because that's all I can say.

↑
cavegirl
Amelia
grunting,
"me, Amelia,
you, Enzo"

He translated for me. I felt kind of dumb having a seven-year-old explain things for me. But then Enzo gave me this note:

DON'T WORRY — SIGNING GETS EASIER WITH PRACTICE. IF YOU LEARN HOW TO SIGN WORDS, NOT JUST SPELL THINGS, IT'LL BE BETTER.

Carlo said that Enzo knows what it's like to want to say more than you can. Enzo gets that feeling himself when people who don't know sign language assume that just because he doesn't use his voice, he doesn't have much to say.

That made me feel better. But if it's this hard learning the alphabet, I don't think I'll EVER be able to sign whole words! The more I learn, the more questions I have. How do you make plurals in sign language? And what about past tense? Are there metaphors, or puns, or funny expressions in sign language? Are there accents? Are there words for loud or quiet — and what do they mean to a deaf person? If I tell Enzo that Cleo snores, will that mean anything to him?

I wish Enzo had questions for me. Maybe he wants to know what certain sounds are like. I could try to make him a mini dictionary of sounds.

BZZZZZZZZZZZ

RRRRRRRRR

yap yap!

barking dog —
sounds like how
quick gasps of air
feel

bees buzzing —
sound like how the
stubble of an
unshaved beard
feels

cat purring —
sounds like how
it feels to wear
a shirt warm from
the dryer

Excuse me!

door slamming —
sounds like how
you feel when you
take a step down
when you weren't
expecting one

burp —
sounds like how
a can of flat,
stale soda tastes

telephone ringing —
sounds like how a
flashing neon light
looks

train whistle —
sounds like how
it feels going
through a long,
dark tunnel, _fast_

the ocean —
sounds like the
feeling of your
heart beating,
but bigger

emergency sirens —
sound like how
it feels to eat
really spicy salsa

# of Sounds
(non-deaf, too)

OOOOAAAA

foghorn—
sounds like
how it feels
going down
an elevator

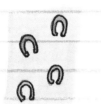

horse hooves clopping—
sound like how a
checkerboard pattern
looks

lips smacking—
sound like
how a dog's
wet nose
feels

baby crying—
sounds like
how rough,
unsanded
wood feels

laughing—
sounds like
how cool
water feels
pouring on you
on a hot day

GNARK!

snoring—
sounds like how
dirty socks smell

pencil on paper—
sounds like how
it feels to walk
barefoot on
sand

HIC!

hiccup—
sounds like
how a belly
button feels
(and looks)

water pouring—
sounds like
the feel of
smooth glass

HOORAY!

cheering crowd—
sounds like how
fireworks look

rubber ducky
squeak—
sounds like
how peppermint
smells (and tastes)

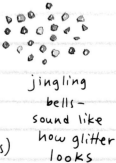

jingling
bells—
sound like
how glitter
looks

I wanted to give Enzo my sound dictionary when I went over there today, but then I was afraid. What if he hated it? What if his feelings were hurt? At least his mom answered a lot of my questions, so I don't feel so dumb. She showed me how Enzo talks to his friends from their old town. He uses a special machine you connect to the phone.

When the door-bell rings, lights flash in different places in the house. But in Enzo's room, there are no flashing lights, so if he was there, he wouldn't know someone was at the door.

It's called a TTY machine. Some are so small you can carry them in a purse!

It works like this: Enzo types in the phone number and message. This is sent to a relay station. The person there calls Enzo's friend, and if the friend can hear, the message is read aloud. If the friend is deaf, the message appears on his own TTY screen.

I hope Enzo doesn't give up on me. I'd like to learn American Sign Language and talk to him the way his family and friends do, but it's hard for me. I'm not even sure how to practice. I'm not used to talking using only my hands — I feel really clumsy and slow. My tongue is so much quicker than my fingers!

Enzo has a pager with a cute, tiny keyboard on it that he uses to send messages — kind of like e-mail. The pager vibrates when there's a message for him.

When I got home, a postcard from Nadia was waiting for me. I love getting mail, especially from Nadia. And postcards are EASY to understand!

Instead of an annoying beep, Enzo's alarm clock has a flashing light.

Dear Amelia,
Sorry to hear Cleo's being so grouchy. I love family gatherings. They're always a lot of fun. I like hearing stories of what my grandparents did when they were kids. And my cousins are great to be with. I just wish we could see each other more often!
How's the sign language going?
Yours till the hand prints, Nadia

38¢
ANTICUS PRIMUS

Amelia
564 North Homecrest
Oopa, Oregon
97881

Too bad learning sign language is <u>slow</u> going. It'd almost be easier to invent my own.

Amelia's Made-Up Signs

It's easier to make up signs of things →

jelly-roll nose—
make a spiral with your pointer finger in front of your nose, then tap your nose

lemon—
pucker those lips!

But how do you sign how you feel about something or describe a dream? ↙

mind your own beeswax—
express yourself with your fingers and tongue

balloon—
fill cheeks with air and look happy (but people might think you're saying "chipmunk")

gross—
lift up one nostril and make an EWW face

I hadn't planned on seeing Enzo today, but when I looked into his backyard, he was there, sitting by the back door. He didn't have to sign anything.

I could tell by the slump of his body that he was really sad.

I leaned over the wall and tossed a pinecone at his feet to get his attention. When he looked up, I waved. He just shrugged, but I came over anyway.

I wanted to cheer up Enzo, but I didn't know how. I couldn't tell jokes in sign language! And I didn't even know what was wrong. Luckily Carlo came out and told me what had happened. This morning their older brother, Gianni, had a bunch of friends over, and Enzo really wanted to join in. At first Gianni signed so Enzo could understand what was going on, but the other kids lost patience with that pretty quickly, and Enzo ended up completely ignored. Kids were laughing and talking all around him, but he felt like a piece of furniture — not like a person at all.

Boy or wallpaper? ↘

Sometimes I feel like I'm hiding behind Carlo because without him, I can't really talk to Enzo. How can I be a good friend if I can't communicate?

I didn't know how to make Enzo feel better. He said sometimes he just hates all hearing people because they're so rude, but when he saw me look sad, he tried to turn it into a joke. "Not you," he signed, "only people who blah blah blah all the time." At least that's what Carlo said Enzo signed — what if Enzo really thinks I'm a blah-blah type person and Carlo is just trying not to hurt my feelings? But I had no choice — I had to trust Carlo to translate.

"Are you mad at Gianni, too?" I asked Enzo, through Carlo.

Enzo shook his head. It wasn't Gianni's fault, he signed. What could he do? Stop being a kid and just be an interpreter?

That made me feel even worse about depending on Carlo to sign for me. Then I remembered the sound dictionary — that could cheer Enzo up! I got it and showed it to him. He didn't think it was stupid — he loved it! At least I don't need Carlo to help me draw.

It's hard for me to imagine what words are like, to someone who can't hear them or feel them in his mouth. For me, some words roll on my tongue like smooth pebbles. Some catch in my throat, some I bite off with my teeth, and some I breathe out. How do words feel if you can't taste them in your mouth? Does poetry work if you can't hear the rhythm and the rhyme? And how do you learn to read in the first place if you can't sound out words?

Some words are like slick stones.

Some are like jingly bells.

Some are sharp as needles.

WEEOoo WEEOoo WEEOoo WEEOoo

Today was the worst day of my life! I had to go to the emergency room, all because of a dried apricot.

Heh, heh, heh

Is it an innocent-looking (though wrinkly) fruit or a health hazard?

I didn't slip on it and crack my head open. I didn't choke on it and need the Heimlich maneuver. All I did was eat it. Mom bought some at the health food store and I'd never tasted one before, so I tried it.

And suddenly I couldn't breathe — I would gulp in air, but it didn't matter. I felt like I was drowning on dry land!

panicked eyes

shocked face

gasping mouth
I didn't even have enough air to say:

HELP!

GENCY!

Luckily my mom took one look at me and knew I was really in trouble. She tried to keep me calm until we got to the hospital. Right away they gave me a shot of something — I was too scared of not breathing to be scared of the needle — and it made me feel better. But here's the bad news — they found out I have asthma. The sulphur in the apricot gave me an asthma attack, and now I have to breathe in all these drugs to keep from having another one.

doctors' room charts — why don't they have <u>interesting</u> things to look at?

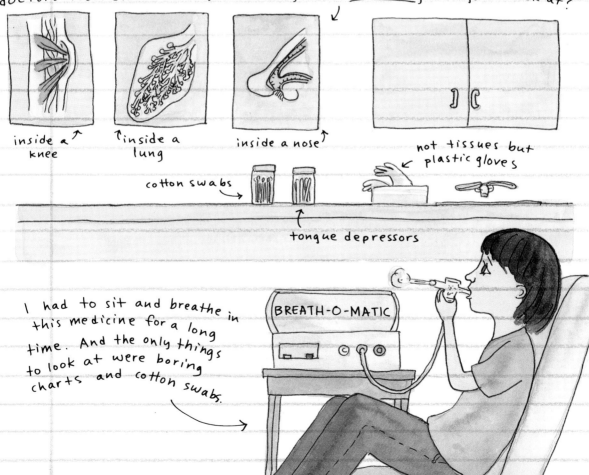

inside a knee

inside a lung

inside a nose

not tissues but plastic gloves

cotton swabs

tongue depressors

I had to sit and breathe in this medicine for a long time. And the only things to look at were boring charts and cotton swabs.

BREATH-O-MATIC

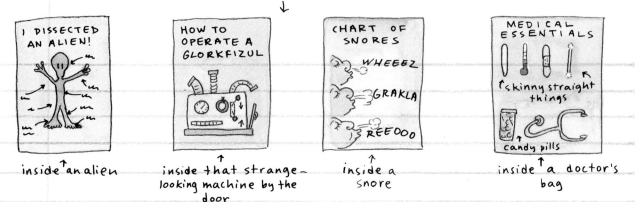

Doctors' room charts I'd like to see:

I DISSECTED AN ALIEN!
inside an alien

HOW TO OPERATE A GLORKFIZUL
inside that strange-looking machine by the door

CHART OF SNORES
WHEEEZ
GRAKLA
REEOOO
inside a snore

MEDICAL ESSENTIALS
skinny straight things
candy pills
inside a doctor's bag

Finally, after I'd memorized the tile pattern on the floor, the doctor said it was O.K. for me to go home, as long as Mom watched me carefully and gave me all my medicine.

So now I'm home, and I feel a lot better. Breathing is still hard work, but at least I can breathe. The thing is, I can't talk well because it takes too much air and it's too exhausting. The doctor said it'll be easier in a week, but for now I can only whisper. When I want something, I write my mom notes.

Please get me the remote control for the TV.

Some juice, please!

Can I have a comic book?

I guess I wrote too many notes, because Mom gave me this one:

YOU CAN STILL WALK — GET YOURSELF JUICE, COMICS, AND THE TV REMOTE!

I could tell it was going to be a looong night!

This morning Enzo came over, and I tried to explain about asthma — as much as I could fit in a small note.

Feel better?

Enzo gave me a get-well card. That was sweet of him.

Carly gave me one yesterday when she visited. →

I've got just the thing to fix 🥄⁇, you up!

I showed Enzo all the medicine I have to take even when I don't feel sick.

↑ The green one tastes O.K.

↑ The blue one is gross.

↑ The white one is nasty!

I admit I was feeling sorry for myself — talking was hard and finger spelling was frustrating and slooow. But even so, being with Enzo made me feel better. I guess we're really friends now.

We had alphabet soup for lunch, and I found the letters very handy. Usually I don't play with my food, but this time I did.

I USE WHAT I CAN TO TALK

Enzo was too hungry to spell with his noodles. He wrote me notes instead (on paper, not soup).

With our family reunion coming up tomorrow, Cleo's been on a huge nagging campaign to get Mom to:
1) let Cleo bring Gigi along, so she won't be bored.
2) let Cleo go to Gigi's house instead, so she won't be bored.

Mom won't even discuss it. She says the choices are:
1) Cleo comes.
2) Cleo comes.

So now Cleo's given up on complicated arguments about free will, child abuse, and children's rights. Now she's just screaming.

I wrote Cleo a note to tell her how Enzo felt left out with Gianni's friends and how lucky she is that people want her around. No one treats _her_ like wallpaper.

"But I WANT to be left out!" she yelled. "I want to be left HOME. Even being able to hear, I'll be just as bored as Enzo was, I know it."

Then I wrote a note about what Nadia had written — how she liked to hear family stories and be with her cousins. But Cleo didn't even read the note. She just stalked off to her room. I was only trying to help. The problem is I don't understand Cleo at all.

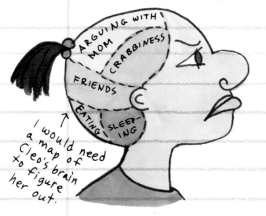

I'm getting kind of excited about the reunion myself. Maybe I'll hear interesting stories. And I can't wait to see my cousin Raisa. She's only four years old, and I haven't seen her since Thanksgiving.

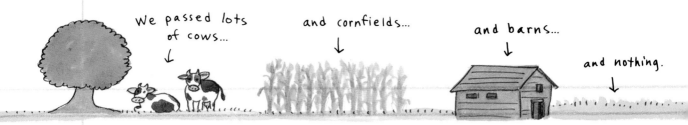

We passed lots of cows... ↓

and cornfields... ↓

and barns... ↓

and nothing. ↓

It was a long drive to Uncle Leroy's farm, and I slept most of the way. Breathing still tires me out, but I'm getting stronger. Mom was in a great mood — she was so excited about seeing everyone. Cleo was in a horrible mood—she was so mad about being forced to go.

she threatened to wear this sign to the reunion. ↘

I AM BEING HELD PRISONER. IT IS _NOT_ MY CHOICE TO BE HERE. RESPECT MY WISHES AND LEAVE ME ALONE!

She scowled the whole way there — but at least she wasn't singing. ↓

At the last minute, she left it in the car, to Mom's relief!

Great-uncles can leap tall silos and stop a tractor. ↑

I didn't know we had such a big family! There were great-uncles and great-aunts I'd never met and cousins once-removed and twice-removed and faraway-removed. There were lots of little kids running around. But Cleo was right — there was no one her age to hang around with. We were the oldest kids there.

My cousin Raisa remembered me! And she talks a lot now. She's not shy like she used to be. But the big surprise was Cleo. All the little kids adored her!

super teeth ↖

Great-great-uncles can do all that, plus have X-ray vision (with their bifocals, of course) and removable teeth!

flowers Raisa picked to give to Cleo →

They all wanted to play with her, show her things, draw pictures for her, and make her mud pies. I think they liked me, too, but since I could only whisper, I was pretty boring to be with.

Cleo was queen for the day. Raisa even made her a glittery crown.

I have to admit, Cleo was great with them. She told jokes, asked funny riddles, and did finger-puppet plays.

She was like the teacher you fall in love with in kindergarten.

I tried to play with my cousins, too, but even drawing pictures didn't interest them for long, because I couldn't tell stories to go with the pictures. Then I tried to show them the sign language alphabet, but they didn't want to see finger spelling — they wanted finger puppets.

My puppets could only dance. They wanted talking puppets. Only Cleo could give them what they wanted.

I tried spending time with the grown-ups, but that wasn't any better. At first, people would ask me how I felt and if I wanted to eat or drink anything, but there wasn't much to say after that, since no one has much patience for hoarse whispers.

Finally, I just sat in a corner and read an old book I found. When I was sick of reading, I watched everyone smiling, laughing, and having a good time. Suddenly I realized that this is what it must be like for Enzo! Only it's worse for him — he can't hear anyone and it's not temporary. It happens every time he's with people who don't know sign language.

Who wants to talk to grown-ups anyway? They ask the same booooring questions all the time!

1. How's school?

2. How's summer?

3. What camp are you going to?

4. My, aren't you growing a lot?

I felt completely invisible — like there was a screen between me and everyone else, just because I couldn't talk! At least, since no one paid any attention to me, I could eavesdrop on all the juicy grown-up gossip. Enzo couldn't even do that.

So it didn't turn out to be exactly the family reunion I'd imagined. But it wasn't what Cleo had dreaded, either. Mom had to drag her away when it was time to go, she was having so much fun.

Cleo got lots of little sticky hugs and kisses.

Bye, Cleo! I wanna be just like you when I'm big.

In fact, Cleo even apologized to Mom when we were driving home!

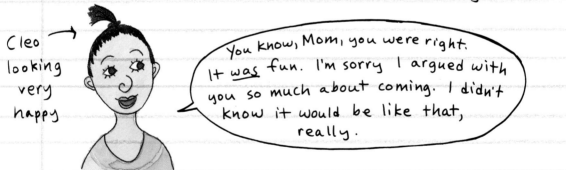

Cleo looking very happy

You know, Mom, you were right. It _was_ fun. I'm sorry I argued with you so much about coming. I didn't know it would be like that, really.

I thought Mom would say, "Nah-nah! I told you so!" But she didn't. She just smiled and said, "I'm so glad you had a good time. I did, too!"

No one asked me what kind of time I had.

← Enzo was sweet! He made me herb tea that he said would help my throat. My throat's not sore — it's my lungs, but I'm better now anyway, and it's the thought that counts.

When I went to Enzo's house today, I told him how sad and left out I felt at the family reunion. And I understood how he felt with Gianni's friends. I wrote how tired I was of using notes and finger spelling to talk with him. I want to talk to him like a _real_ friend.

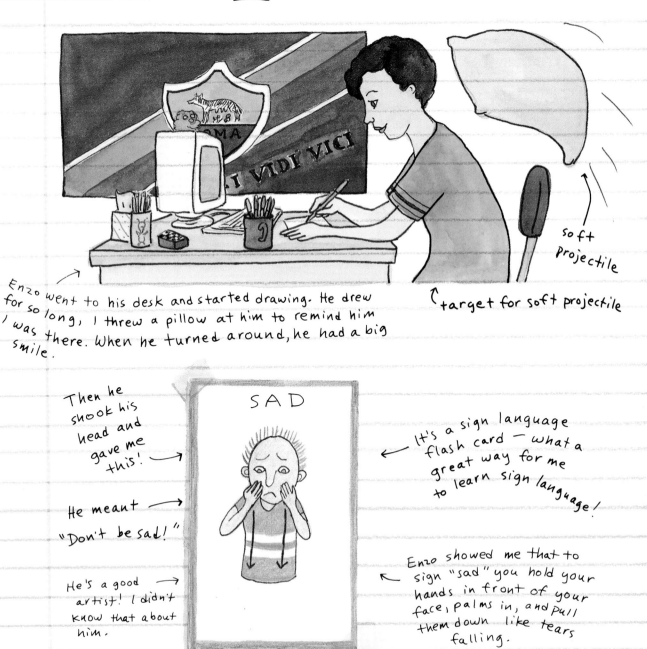

Enzo went to his desk and started drawing. He drew for so long, I threw a pillow at him to remind him I was there. When he turned around, he had a big smile.

soft projectile

↳ target for soft projectile

SAD

Then he shook his head and gave me this! →

He meant → "Don't be sad!"

He's a good → artist! I didn't know that about him.

← It's a sign language flash card — what a great way for me to learn sign language!

↖ Enzo showed me that to sign "sad" you hold your hands in front of your face, palms in, and pull them down like tears falling.

I thought it was such a great idea, I wanted to make more cards. Together, we ended up making 10 cards today. I'd write down a word I wanted to learn, Enzo would sign it, and I drew the picture. Then we'd practice a few times with each card. I feel like I'm finally learning sign language! Soon Enzo and I will really be able to talk to each other — without notes or Carlo translating.

Some signs look like what they are — for "banana" you pretend to peel a banana.

↑ finger banana

For "ice cream" you lick an imaginary cone.

Signs for ideas aren't as easy to remember, but they can be like beautiful hand dances.

And the great thing is that with signs, I don't have to worry about spelling! This is the sign for ~~wierd~~ ~~weird~~ ~~wierd~~ weird — the letters don't matter. I just have to make a face like I smell something strange.

Make your hand into a C, then drop it in front of your shoulder.

I can't wait to learn "invent" and "dream" and "together." There are so many words I want to know! I have lots to say and so does Enzo.

I learned the sign for "when." I wanted to know when we could make more flash cards.

Your pointer finger makes a clockwise circle around your other upright pointer finger (like the earth rotating). Then touch those fingers together.

The thumb touches your cheek and arcs forward — that means "tomorrow!"

When I got home, I wrote a story.

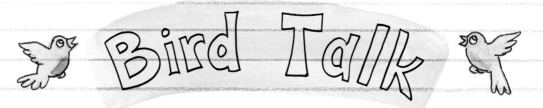

Bird Talk

bird
tracks
↓

Once there was a girl who could talk to birds. She understood all their songs and whistles and chirps. Even without having a beak, she could sing just like them.

The birds would tell her about what they'd seen in their travels, where the best berries grew, and how to find secret caves. The girl would tell them about the strange things humans do, like read newspapers, take buses, and play soccer.

Have you heard the one about the robin?

Then one day a wise owl heard about the girl. He asked blue jays, sparrows, and wrens where she was, until he found her.

Finally!

I've been looking everywhere!

But he hadn't come all that long way for a chance to talk to a person. Instead, he said, "It's time for you to choose between bird language and human talk. You can't do both anymore." He showed her two seeds—one bright red and shiny like a jewel, and one dull and black like coal.

"If you eat the red one," said the owl, "you will sing like a bird, but you won't be able to speak to people. If you eat the black one, you will talk like a human, but not chirp like a bird. You must decide which world you want to belong in."

"Why can't I do both, like I do now — and like you do?" asked the girl.

The owl ruffled his feathers, annoyed.

"I'm a special case — you're not," he harrumphed. "Besides, your time is up."

"No, it's not!" said the girl. Quick as a wink, she grabbed the seeds and swallowed them both.

Gulp!

"NO!" yelled the owl. But it was too late.

The girl smiled. "I guess I have more time after all. Don't worry, I'll use it wisely." And she did.

The girl even learned to speak cat and dog. As for the owl, he didn't stay mad at the girl. He liked talking to her too much himself — in both bird AND human talk.

The End

Seen any good fish lately?

No, but there's a great fire hydrant down the block.

I don't usually show my notebook to anyone, but I decided to let Enzo read my bird story. I thought he would think it was ~~wierd~~ ~~weird~~ ~~wierd~~ weird, but after he read it, he smiled and made this sign:

If only I could use sign language for this word ALL the time!

The pointer finger and thumb of the top hand make a half circle and then tap the thumb and pointer finger of the bottom hand.

It means "perfect!"

I guess Enzo understood my story. That's another great thing about writing and drawing — you don't need to hear to do them. I'm excited that I not only have a new friend, I'm learning a cool, new language. So I'll keep working on my sign language flash cards. Enzo helped me make some terrific ones today. Now I know how to sign "private," "keep out," and "top-secret notebook." Or I can just do it the old-fashioned way, with a drawing.

Amazing how much you can communicate with your face.

sign for "thank you"

Touch your hand to your mouth, then lower your hand to waist level.

sign for "friend"

Lock your pointer fingers together. Take them apart and turn your hands over and lock your fingers again.